Robbers of the Giant Cactus

Elaine Pageler

High Noon Books
Novato, California

D0029530

Cover Design: Jill Zwicky
Interior Illustrations: Tina Cash-Walsh

International Standard Book Number: 1-57128-002-2

6 5 4 3 2 1 0 9 8 7
1 0 9 8 7 6 5 4 3 2

Contents

1 Land of the Saguaros 1

2 A Problem at the Ranch........................7

3 Plans for Morning...............................14

4 The Saguaro Harvest 19

5 The Suspects......................................27

6 More Red Ribbons..............................32

7 Catching the Robbers 38

Nate and Nell's mother is an ecology professor. During the year, Dr. Kidd teaches at a college. When summer comes, people invite her to meetings all around the country. Nate and Nell often travel with her.

"Ecology is man and nature living together in harmony," their mother always says.

Nate and Nell smile. "And we're the Kidds who help," they say.

CHAPTER 1

Land of the Saguaros (sah-WAR-ohs)

The Kidd's plane skimmed over the ground. They were about to land at Tucson, Arizona.

Nate stared down at the desert below. "Look at all those tall green things. They're growing everywhere," he said.

His twin sister Nell leaned forward. "Yes, they look like a forest of people. What are they, Mom?" she asked.

"They're saguaros, the largest cactus in the United States," their mother told them.

Just then Nate felt a bump. The plane had touched down.

Dr. Kidd closed her briefcase. "My meetings are in Tucson. But we're staying at a guest ranch in the desert. You two will like it," she said.

"Will they send someone to pick us up?" Nate asked.

"Should I take out my 'Ecology Kidds' sign? Then they'll know who we are," Nell said.

"No, I rented a car. Two of the Saguaro National Monuments are near Tucson. They have great groves of saguaros. I'll have spare time. We'll drive out to see them," Dr. Kidd said.

The plane taxied to a stop. The Kidds got off and went to get their luggage.

"Stay with the bags. I'll get the car," Mom told Nate and Nell.

They didn't have to wait long. Soon their mother drove up in a blue car. They loaded their bags and got in.

Dr. Kidd drove down the freeway. After a while, she turned onto a narrow road. The desert was on both sides.

Nate couldn't believe his eyes. The giant cactus grew everywhere. Most of the tall ones had arms that pointed upward.

Nell pushed her nose against the window. "The saguaros are really tall!" she gasped.

Dr. Kidd nodded. "Some saguaros grow 50 feet tall. They can live for 200 years," she said.

"Wow, that's old. Why do they have holes in their trunks?" Nate asked.

"I just saw a bird fly out of one hole," Nell added.

Their mother stopped the car on the side of the road. Then she got out and walked into the saguaros. Nate and Nell followed.

Mom pointed to the holes. "The Gila (HEE-la) woodpeckers made those. That's where they make their nests. It's much cooler in the saguaro than out in the sun. The woodpeckers leave after their babies are born. Then others move into the cool homes."

Nate mopped his forehead. "That sounds smart to me. The desert gets hot," he said.

"Who moves in?" Nell wanted to know.

"Elfin owls make nests in the holes. So do flycatchers, warblers, martins, finches and starlings. Wrens, doves and hawks use the saguaro, too. They build nests where the arms of the saguaro poke out from the trunk," their mother told them.

"Wow, lots of birds depend on saguaros," Nate said.

Mom nodded. "They are important to life in the desert. Without saguaros, many living things would die," she said.

Nell pointed to another saguaro. It was brown instead of green. "What's wrong with this one?" she asked.

"It looks as if it's dying," Nate said.

Dr. Kidd agreed. "Saguaros have many enemies. It could have been a late frost. Perhaps it's pollution. Or maybe it was struck by lightning."

The Kidds went back to their car. They drove up the road. Around the bend sat a sheriff's car. Its lights were flashing.

Mom stopped and rolled down the window. "What's wrong?" she asked.

The sheriff pointed to two holes in the ground. "Saguaro robbers have struck again. This is the second time this week," he said.

Dr. Kidd turned to Nate and Nell. A sad look was on her face. "Now you know another enemy of the saguaro. It's greedy men," she said.

CHAPTER 2

A Problem at the Ranch

Dr. Kidd drove on down the road. This part had many potholes. Everyone jiggled around.

Nell hung on to the seat. "This road needs to be fixed," she said.

Nate hung on, too. But his mind was still on what the sheriff had said. "Is there a law against stealing saguaros?" he asked.

"Yes, years ago people started taking lots of saguaros. So the law was passed. Now a person must have a permit to dig one," Dr. Kidd said.

"I guess there are saguaro robbers around here," Nate said.

Their mother nodded. "The law stopped most of the stealing. But there is always a market for saguaros. Some greedy people think only of making money," she said.

"The robbers don't think of the birds. The poor things lose their homes," Nell said.

Mom slowed down and turned onto a narrow lane. It wound through the desert.

"Look," Nate said. He pointed to some red tiled roofs peeking above the brush.

"That's the guest ranch. It's managed by the Rivas. They're friends of mine. They have a son about your age," Dr. Kidd said.

She stopped in front of an iron gate. It opened into a courtyard of trees and flowers. A low adobe (uh-DOH-bee) building surrounded it on three sides. There was a fountain in the middle.

The Kidds got out and walked into the lobby. The walls were white with dark beams going across the ceiling.

"Oh, it's nice and cool in here," Nell said.

A man and a boy stood behind the counter. Nate thought the boy was about his age.

The man saw them and smiled. "You must be Dr. Kidd and the twins. Welcome to Cactus Land Guest Ranch. My name is Tom. Mr. and Mrs. Riva said to make you welcome. They're

A man and a boy stood behind the counter.

away on a business trip," he said.

Mom's smile faded. "I'm sorry to miss them," she said.

The boy cut in. "You won't. My parents will be back in three days. I'm Josh. They left me in charge of making your trip fun. Do you like to hike?" he asked Nate and Nell.

"Hold on, Josh. Give them a chance to get into their rooms. You can talk about hiking at dinner," the man said.

Josh's dark eyes sparkled. "O.K., here are your keys. I'll help with your bags," he said.

The Kidds had three rooms. All opened onto a patio that looked out on the courtyard. Nate chose a room and started unpacking.

"Tap, tap," came a sound from the patio.

Nell was knocking on his door. She pointed to the parking lot. "The sheriff's car just drove up. I wonder what he wants," she said.

Nate stepped out on the patio. He saw Tom in the garden inspecting the flowers.

The sheriff went over to him. "Where are Mr. and Mrs. Riva?" he asked.

"Mr. and Mrs. Riva are gone. They left last night," Tom told him.

"Where did they go?" the sheriff asked.

"It's a business trip. Mr. and Mrs. Riva drove their van to the airport. Then they flew to the West Coast. It's too bad they had to go now. Dr. Kidd and her children came today. She is

12

their friend," Tom said.

The sheriff told him about the missing saguaros. "This looks bad. The Riva van was seen last night. It was at the spot where the saguaros were taken. Then they leave town. The saguaros could have been in their van," he said.

Tom looked shocked. "I don't think the Rivas would steal saguaros," he said.

"I hope not. But keep your eyes open. Call me if anything else happens," the sheriff said.

The sheriff went to his car. Tom walked inside.

That's when Nate saw a shadow move in a doorway. Someone else had been listening.

"It's Josh," Nell whispered.

CHAPTER 3

Plans for the Morning

The dining room was crowded that night. But Josh had saved a place for the Kidds.

He looked at Nate and Nell. "Now I'll ask you again. Do you like hiking? I've got a good one planned for tomorrow," he said.

"You bet we do," Nate told him.

"Where are we going?" Nell asked.

Josh pointed out the window. "My aunt and uncle are harvesting saguaros tomorrow. They'll be on the other side of that ridge," he said.

"I didn't know people harvested saguaros," Nate said.

"Do you mean people eat them?" Nell asked.

Josh nodded. "Saguaros are very important to my mother's people. She's from the Tohono O'odham (toh-HO-no o-O-dahm) Indian tribe. Their reservation is near here," he said.

Tom entered the room with a portable telephone. "Josh, your parents are on the line. They want to talk to you," he said.

Josh talked for a while. Then he hung up.

"Mom and Dad said to tell you hi, Dr. Kidd," he said.

Tom had remained at the table. "What did they want? Is anything wrong?" he asked.

Josh shook his head. "They called to find out how the building went today," he said.

"What building?" Nate's mother asked.

"They're building several new condos out in back. So we've had workers all summer. I told Mom and Dad two more condos were done. The carpet layers will be out tomorrow," Josh said.

Just then the door opened. The sheriff walked in. Nate saw the smile leave Josh's face. All the people got quiet. They turned toward the sheriff.

He looked around the room. "I just came to tell you about the main road. They'll be working on it tomorrow," he said.

"That road needs work," Nell whispered.

"So the road will be closed for a couple of days," the sheriff went on.

Dr. Kidd spoke up. "Is there another road? I need to go to an ecology meeting tomorrow," she said.

"I'm going to it, too," another man said.

"I suggest you get together and take one car. You can get through the detour. I will have a deputy at the end of your lane. He will direct you," the sheriff said.

Mom talked to the other man. "He has a jeep. I'll leave my car in the parking lot," she told Nate and Nell.

"Park it under the mesquite (mess-KEET) tree. It's cooler there," Josh said.

After dinner Mom and the twins parked the car under the tree. It sloped down. Mom set the brakes. Below them was a road and bridge leading behind the buildings.

Dr. Kidd went to her room. But Nate and Nell went to the lobby. They wanted to talk to Josh.

Nate opened the door. Josh stood at the counter. His back was to them. "I thought you would want to know, Dad," he said into the phone.

Nate and Nell looked at each other. They tiptoed back out.

"Why did Josh phone his Dad again?" Nell asked.

Nate frowned. "I don't know," he said.

CHAPTER 4

The Saguaro Harvest

Nate and Nell met Josh after breakfast. They had canteens and wore hats and long-sleeved shirts.

Josh eyed their canteens. "Good, you'll need water. It's going to be hot today. First we go down Old Road," he told them.

Old Road went over the bridge and behind the buildings. Off to one side were the new condos. Nate saw two trucks parked nearby. They must belong to the workers inside.

The road went on toward the long, flat mountain. Nate didn't see any tire tracks. This part must not be used much. They followed the road until it came to a dry creek bed.

Josh pointed to it. "We call that dry creek a 'wash,' " he said.

Now the road turned and followed the wash downhill.

Josh stepped off the road. "We'll hike up the wash. It will lead us up to the top of the ridge," he said.

Nell pointed to three saguaros that stood close together. "Here's our family. The tall one is Mom. The two shorter ones are twins just like Nate and me," she said.

Nell pointed to three saguaros.
"Here's our family."

Nate spotted a red ribbon on each of the smaller ones. "What's that for?" he asked.

Josh shook his head. "I've never seen that before. Come on, let's go."

At first the wash was mostly sand. But it got rocky as they went higher. Now walking was harder, and the sun became hotter, too.

Josh reached for his canteen. "It's time for water. Drink even though you may not be thirsty. Your body needs it," he told them.

After that they went on walking. Soon they reached the top of the ridge.

Josh pointed down the slope. "There's some of my family now," he said.

Nate could see some pickups far below

them. There were people nearby.

Josh hurried down the slope. Nate and Nell followed him.

Now Nate could see the people better. They were women and children. Some of the women had long poles. Crosspieces were nailed to the tops. They used these poles to pull down the fruit growing high on the saguaros.

The children tried to catch the fruit. They took it over to the buckets. A woman scooped out the red pulp and the tiny black seeds. She dropped the outside hulls on the ground.

Josh waved his hand. "Hi, Auntie. Hi, everyone. This is Nate and Nell," he called.

"Hi, Nate and Nell," everyone said.

The women went back to work. Nell walked over to the buckets. She tried scooping out pulp and seeds. Then she threw the hull down.

Josh shook his head. "The hull needs to be face up. That's my family's offering for rain."

The women stopped at 10 o'clock. "It's time to go back to camp," they said.

Everyone took the buckets and headed for the pickup trucks.

Josh climbed in the back of a pickup and signaled to Nate and Nell. "Come on," he said.

The campsite wasn't far away. The men had fires burning. They took the buckets from the pickups.

The saguaro pulp was mixed with water. Then it was put on the fire. Meanwhile Josh, Nate, and Ned talked with Josh's family.

"The saguaro has always been our friend," his aunt said.

"It fed our people before they learned to farm," his uncle added.

"Birds like the fruit, too. So do the coyote and the javelina (hav-a-LEEN-a) and other animals. Insects eat it, too. The saguaro feeds all of us," Josh said.

Soon it was lunchtime and everyone ate.

By now the fruit had cooked a long time. The women poured it through a mesh. That kept the pulp and seeds from the juice.

"We will put the pulp and seeds in the sun to dry. Later we will make candy, jams, and syrups from them," the aunt said.

After that the uncle drove Josh, Nate, and Nell back to the ridge. They climbed over the top and walked down the wash.

Nate could see the road ahead. That meant they were almost back.

"Look, the twins are gone!" Nell cried.

She pointed to the side of the wash. Three saguaros had been there this morning. Now only the tall one was left. Two holes were beside it.

Nate looked at Josh. "The saguaro robbers have struck again," he said.

Josh nodded. His face had turned pale.

CHAPTER 5

The Suspects

Nate pointed to the ground near the missing saguaros. "Here are footprints. I think two people were here," he said.

Josh nodded. He followed the footprints out to the road. "There are tire tracks, too. They weren't here this morning. The robbers loaded the saguaros in a truck," he said.

"Or a van," Nate added.

"The main road is closed. My mother and father are right," Josh said.

"What do you mean?" Nate asked.

"There have been some saguaro robberies lately. Mom and Dad think it's someone from the ranch. There have been lots of people working on the new condos," Josh said.

Nate and Nell exchanged glances. Both of them remembered the sheriff's visit. He thought Josh's parents were guilty.

Josh went on. "Dad discovered two missing saguaros. This was when he was checking the ranch just before they left on their trip," he said.

"Did he phone the sheriff? That's what I would do if I discovered missing saguaros," Nell said.

Josh shook his head. "They didn't have

time to wait for the sheriff. Their plane was leaving in an hour. So they decided to report it when they got back. They'd only be gone for three days."

"Well, the robbers struck again. Where does this road go?" Nate asked.

"This road doesn't go anywhere. It stops in another mile. The robbers would have to go past the house to get out," Josh told them.

Nell's eyes lit up. "Then they'd need to use the main road. The sheriff's deputy is there. He'd see anyone coming out," she said.

"You're right," Josh said.

They hurried back to the ranch. Tom stood at the counter. He looked up as they came in.

"Two more of our saguaros have been stolen," Josh called.

Tom looked shocked as he heard their story. Then he called the sheriff and told him what had happened.

Tom put down the phone. "This has been a bad day. The carpet layers brought out one roll of wrong carpet. So they couldn't finish today. Now there's this," he said.

The sheriff arrived in a few minutes. "Tell me about the missing saguaros," he said.

Nate told him what happened. "It's where Old Road meets the wash," he said.

"It happened today. My parents are away. That should prove they're not the saguaro robbers," Josh said.

"Maybe not. Perhaps they hired someone to steal the saguaros today. That would make them look innocent," the sheriff said.

"My parents aren't robbers. I'm going to prove it," Josh said. He walked away.

The sheriff watched him go. Then he went to his truck. Tom left, too.

"I believe Josh. His mother wouldn't do that. She's an Indian. Indians know that saguaros are their friends," Nell said.

Nate nodded. "We've got to help Josh catch the real thieves," he said.

CHAPTER 6

Red Ribbons

The sheriff arrived at breakfast the next morning. "We searched the ranch and found nothing. Two cars went out yesterday afternoon. One was the carpenters. The other belonged to the carpet layers. Both cars were searched. No saguaros were found," he told them.

"What happens now?" Josh asked.

"There'll be a 24-hour watch on the road. We'll get them," the sheriff said.

Josh bent his head toward Nate and Nell.

"The saguaros must be hidden somewhere. The sheriff isn't good at searching the desert. But I am. Do you want to help me?" he asked.

"Sure," they said.

"O.K., here's my idea. Nell will stay and watch the ranch. Nate and I will search for the saguaros in the desert," Josh said.

An hour later, Nate and Josh were walking up Old Road again.

"Saguaros are very heavy. Their skin swells when it rains. Extra water is stored inside," Josh said.

"I guess the saguaro has its own canteen," Nate said.

"That's right and it's a big one. Full-grown

saguaros can weigh several tons. Of course, these were much smaller ones. Still, they're too heavy to carry far," Josh said.

"Then we should look for footprints that lead off this road," Nate said.

"That's right," Josh said.

The boys walked to the end of the road. They found no saguaros.

"Maybe the saguaros are hidden in the ranch buildings or the new condos," Nate suggested.

"No, I've already looked there," Josh said.

Nate spotted something up ahead. "Look, there are ribbons on two more saguaros. They're like the ones we saw yesterday," he said.

Josh's eyes widened. "It must be a signal. These saguaros will be stolen, too. Go phone the sheriff. I'll stay here and watch," he said.

Nate started walking. He got tired and hot. There was a cliff off to the side. He walked to it and sat in the shade for a few minutes. Suddenly he heard a motor. He raced back to the road.

He was too late. All he saw was a cloud of dust heading toward the saguaros and Josh.

Nate raced down the road. Finally the ranch came into view.

Tom was in the lobby. He looked up and spotted Nate's red face. "You look hot. Have you been hiking?" he asked.

"Yes," Nate gasped.

Nate was too late. All he saw was a cloud of dust heading toward the saguaros and Josh.

He told Tom about the red ribbons and the motor he heard. "We think those saguaros will be stolen. Will you phone the sheriff?" he asked.

"Sure, I'll do it right now," Tom said.

Nate rushed out of the lobby. He raced down the road again. Josh might need his help.

Once again Nate heard a truck. This time it headed toward him. He couldn't see it yet. But it was coming fast.

Nate jumped off the road. A minute later the carpet layers' truck whizzed by.

Someone came running up the road. It was Josh. "Stop them, they're the saguaro robbers," he called.

CHAPTER 7

Catching the Robbers

Josh ran up to Nate. "I watched the carpet layers dig up the saguaros. They wrapped them in a roll of carpet," he said.

"They won't get away. The sheriff is on his way," Nate told him.

"Did you phone him?" Josh asked.

"No. Tom said he would. I hurried back to help you," Nate said.

"Oh, no, not Tom!" Josh exclaimed.

"Why not?" asked Nate.

"I could hear the carpet layers talking. They said Tom marked the saguaros. He's part of their gang," Josh told him.

Nate's smile changed to a frown. "Then Tom won't call the sheriff. They'll get away."

"Yeah. I'm the one who saw them dig up the saguaros. The sheriff won't believe me. He'll think I'm trying to help my parents," Josh said.

"I'm sorry," said Nate.

"It's not your fault. You didn't know about Tom," Josh said.

They went on walking. But there was no hurry now. The robbers would get away before they could get to a phone.

The boys came around a bend.

"Look!" Josh shouted.

The carpet layers' truck was backing up. It was coming toward them. The boys jumped out of the way. It screeched by.

"What's happening? Why are they going backward?" Nate asked.

Josh pointed toward the ranch. "Look! The bridge is blocked. They can't get through."

Nate looked in that direction. Their mother's rental car sat in the middle of the bridge.

"How did it get there?" Nate asked.

"Who knows? We've got to follow the carpet layers," Josh said.

The boys turned and raced down the road. At last they found the truck. It was parked near where the saguaros had been taken.

"They're putting them back," Nate said.

"The bridge is blocked. They don't want to be caught with the saguaros," Josh said.

The boys tiptoed closer. They peeked around a cactus. The men worked fast. They were putting the saguaros back in the holes.

"Wooooh," came a siren. The sheriff's truck roared toward them. He and his deputies jumped out. Tom was with them. He wore handcuffs.

The carpet layers started making excuses. "We found these saguaros behind the condos. They might die. So we brought them out here," one of them said.

41

Josh jumped out of his hiding place. "That's not true. I saw them dig up the saguaros," he said.

The sheriff patted Josh's arm. "I know. Tom has confessed. Your parents aren't guilty. We caught the real robbers thanks to Nell."

"Do you mean my sister?" Nate gasped.

"That's right. She blocked the bridge and phoned me," the sheriff said.

The whole story came out at dinner that night. The sheriff sat at the table with Dr. Kidd, the twins, and Josh.

First the boys told their story. Then Nell told hers.

"The carpet layers' truck went down Old

Road. I went to tell Tom. But Nate was talking to him. I heard Tom promise Nate to phone the sheriff. But he called the carpet store instead."

"So you blocked the bridge," Nate said.

Nell glanced at Mom. "I had to do something. So I took off the brake and steered the car onto the bridge. Then I phoned the sheriff," she said.

"That was fast thinking," Mom told her.

"My men went to the carpet store. The other saguaros were hidden in carpet rolls. That's how they got past my deputy. We've planted the saguaros back in the desert," the sheriff said.

"Good! Lots of birds, animals and insects

will depend on them," Nate said.

Dr. Kidd nodded. "Saguaros depend on others, too. It's Mother Nature at work. Birds, bees, and bats carry pollen from one saguaro flower to another. This causes seeds. Animals move the seeds to other places. Termites and other insects eat the dead saguaros so they don't litter the desert," she said.

Nate looked at his mother. "It sounds as if everyone helps everyone else. What can people do for the saguaro?" he asked.

"Just help to keep them safe," Mom said.

"I guess we did that today," Nell said.

Her mother grinned. "You certainly did," she said.